Snowed In!

By Sierra Harimann
Illustrated by The Artifact Group

SCHOLASTIC INC.

ISBN 978-0-545-47233-3

12 11 10 9 8 7 6 5 4 3 2 1 12 13 14 15 16 17/0

Printed in the U.S.A. 40

Designed by Angela Jun
First printing, December 2012

A gust of cold air blew into Puppyville Manor as Fuji and Spike returned from the movies one afternoon.

"Quick, close the door," Spike barked to Fuji. "It's cold out there!"

"You're in luck," Montana told her friends. "I just made a pot of tea and some snacks. Would you like some?"

"Yes, please!" Fuji said. "I'd love something to warm me up."

Montana poured the tea for her friends.

"I'm so excited that it's cold outside!" she yipped happily.

"Why on earth would you be glad about the cold?" grumbled Spike. "I hate winter."

"My aunt Eleanor is coming to visit this weekend," Montana explained. "She's bringing her twin puppies, Lenny and Maxwell, and I hope it snows. I really want to build a snow fort and have a snowball fight."

"Sounds like fun!" Fuji told her friend. "When do they get here?"

"Tomorrow night," Montana replied. "They're staying at the Snowy Peaks Lodge on the other side of the mountain pass. There's a fantastic hill for sledding there."

"I'll keep my paws crossed that it snows, then," Spike said, even though he preferred beach weather.

Montana and Fuji headed to the kitchen to wash the dishes.

"Did I hear that we're having visitors?" Gigi asked.

"We are," Montana barked cheerfully.

"Then we'll need to have some treats on hand!" Gigi replied. "I'm on my way out. I can pick up some croissants and éclairs at the Barkery if you want."

"Or I can help you bake something homemade, Montana," Fuji said. "We can make my famous snowball cookies. Maybe that will help your wish come true."

"Thanks, Fuji!" Montana barked. "That sounds great."

A few hours later, the cookies were cooling and Montana was getting ready for bed. She knew she was going to have trouble falling asleep, because she was so excited to see her aunt and her cousins the next day.

The next morning, Montana woke up and rushed to the window. A thick blanket of white covered the ground, and sparkly icicles hung from the trees.

"Yippee!" Montana yelped loudly. "It snowed! My wish came true!"

"You might want to see this, Montana," Freddy said as he gestured toward the TV.

"Due to the heavy snowfall, Mountain Pass Road will be closed until further notice," the weather puppy announced.

Montana's face fell.

"Oh, no," she said sadly. "Mountain Pass Road is the only way in and out of Puppyville! Aunt Eleanor, Lenny, and Maxwell will never get here now."

The other puppies tried to cheer Montana up.

"We can build a snowpuppy right here in front of Puppyville Manor!" Spike said.

"And we can build a fort and have a snowball fight, too," Sammy added. "It will be fun."

Montana sighed.

"Thanks, guys," she said. "But it just won't be the same without my cousins. I've been looking forward to seeing them so much."

A few hours later, Speckles and Dottie stopped by to invite Montana and some of the other puppies to go ice skating on the lake.

"Thanks for the invitation," Montana told her friends, "but I'm not in the mood for skating."

"Are you sure?" Speckles asked. "The lake's frozen solid, and the fresh snow will make things extra pretty. Come on, it will be fun!"

"My aunt and my cousins were coming to visit all the way from New Paw City, but Mountain Pass Road is closed," Montana explained. "I don't think they'll be able to get here, but I have to wait to see what happens."

Ring, ring!

It was Montana's cell phone.

"Hello?" Montana said. "Hi, Aunt Eleanor."

She paused.

"I'm not sure, but I can try," Montana finally said before she hung up the phone.

"Who was that?" Spike asked.

"It was my aunt," Montana replied. "She and the puppies made it to the Snowy Peaks Lodge. But because the road is closed, they can't go any farther. She asked if there's any way I can get there to visit with them, but I just don't see how."

"Wait a minute!" Speckles suddenly said. "I know what you can do! Dottie and I just got skis last week. You can borrow mine and ski over the mountain pass!"

"Great idea, Speckles," Dottie told her brother.

"*Hmmm,*" Montana said. "That might work, except I don't know how to ski!"

"Dottie's a great skier," Speckles said. "I bet she'll go with you and she'll teach you, right, Dottie?"

"Of course!" Dottie barked happily.

"Really?" Montana asked. "You'd do that for me? Thanks, Dottie!"

"My pleasure," Dottie said. "Speckles and I will go grab the skis while you pack and get ready to go. We'll be back soon!"

Montana pulled on a warm jacket, earmuffs, and mittens so she would be warm on her way to Snowy Peaks Lodge.

"Don't forget the snowball cookies we made!" Fuji said as she packed them up in a box. "You should bring them to share with your aunt and cousins."

"Thanks, Fuji!" Montana barked. "You're the best."

Montana and Dottie headed out as soon as they could. Dottie gave Montana pointers the whole way.

"Bend your knees a little bit," Dottie said. "And keep your skis next to each other. Now just glide back and forth. Watch your balance!"

"Um . . . okay," Montana said as she pushed off with one ski. "Here goes!"

"That's it!" Dottie encouraged her. "You're doing great! We'll be there in no time."

"Wow!" Montana said breathlessly as she and Dottie skied up to the Snowy Peaks Lodge. "That was really fun! Thank you so much for helping me today. I learned how to ski, *and* I get to see my aunt and cousins!"

"Montana!" Lenny cried. "You made it! Did you ski all the way here from Puppyville?"

"Wow!" Maxwell added.

Aunt Eleanor laughed. "Settle down, boys, settle down," she said. "Montana, it's so good to see you."

"And it's great to see all of you!" Montana barked.
Montana, Lenny, and Maxwell spent the rest of the afternoon building a snowpuppy. It looked so real that the squirrels were afraid to go near it.

Meanwhile, Dottie showed Aunt Eleanor how to ski.

"Oh, my!" Aunt Eleanor cried as she skied down a small hill. "*Wheee!* "

Everyone laughed. Then they all headed inside for some warm milk and snowball cookies.

It was the perfect end to Montana's perfect snow day full of friends, fun, and family!